Then the kidnappers forced Barbara into a large hole in the ground. There were still piles of dirt on the ground next to it. From the amount of dirt visible, Barbara knew the hole was deep.

"I want you to slide down in there," the man said, pressing hard on Barbara's shoulder to push her in.

Terrified at the thought of being buried alive, she struggled to get free. But the man was too strong for her, and in seconds she was forced into the hole and underground "room."

But she found no "room" at the bottom of the hole. The man had lied to her. It was a box barely large enough for her to sit up in. She was sealed inside a coffin! There was no way she could survive seven days in here. She tried to get up, to get out of the hole. "No!" she shouted. "No!"

But it was too late. The man slammed the lid of the box and Barbara was plunged into total darkness.

She heard dirt falling on top of the box, filling up the hole. She was being buried alive!

TRUE FRIGHT
Buried Alive!
and Other True Stories Scarier than Fiction

Ted Pedersen

TOR®

A TOM DOHERTY ASSOCIATES BOOK
NEW YORK

TRUE FRIGHT: BURIED ALIVE! AND OTHER TRUE STORIES SCARIER THAN FICTION

Cover illustration by Robert Papp

A Tor Book
Published by Tom Doherty Associates, Inc.
175 Fifth Avenue
New York, N.Y. 10010

Tor® is a registered trademark of Tom Doherty Associates, Inc.

ISBN: 0-812-54396-3

First edition: August 1996

Printed in the United States of America

0 9 8 7 6 5 4 3 2 1

To Ruth Maxwell

Acknowledgments

The author wishes to acknowledge the invaluable assistance of Francis Moss in making this book happen, and a special thanks to Steve Hayes for revealing a "true fright" from his own family history.

Contents

Introduction

Someone once said, "Truth is stranger than fiction." Perhaps that's true, but let me add this: "Truth is also *scarier* than fiction."

These stories, like those in *True Fright: Volume One*, are attempts to prove the latter theory.

This book, as with the earlier collection, *True Fright: Volume One*, will attempt to prove this theory.

All of the stories are frightening—blood-curdling, to be precise. And all of them are true.

Though you may find these tales unbelievable, they are not make-believe. All events in this book happened—or so we are told by those who were there.

There are many ways to be frightened. You

might see a ghost haunting a beautiful home in Beverly Hills, or spend a fearful night in an isolated cottage on a Scottish beach, or suddenly find yourself in a terrible natural disaster like a flood or fire. Or, more horrifyingly, be buried alive.

And, though you're probably reading these stories in the safety of your home, you may still feel the dread that is at the heart of each True Fright!

The Girl Who Was
Buried Alive

Claustrophobia is the fear of being trapped in small spaces. A person may become frightened in an elevator, or when locked in a small room. But that is minor compared to what happened to a college student named Barbara—she was buried alive.

It began two weeks before Christmas 1968. Barbara Mackle was a student at Emory University in Atlanta, and her holiday enthusiasm was dampened by a bad case of the flu. Her mother was concerned enough to fly up from her home in Miami. She rented a room at a local motel, where Barbara soon joined her. Barbara's mother took care of her while she rested and studied for exams.

Early on a Tuesday morning there was a

sharp knock on their door. Barbara was half asleep when she heard her mother treading across the room to the door. She could hear only her mother's half of the conversation.

"Oh, no," Barbara's mother said worriedly. She turned to look at Barbara, who was beginning to sit up in bed. "It's a policeman," Barbara's mother said. "Stewart's been in an accident."

Stewart was a close friend of Barbara's who attended college with her.

As her mother started to unbolt the door, Barbara felt a sudden shiver of uncertainty. Something wasn't right. "Mother, don't . . ."

But it was too late. The man behind the door used his weight to force it open, knocking Barbara's mother backward.

Suddenly he was standing in the room. Barbara saw that he held what seemed to be a gun. Behind him, another man, shorter and smaller, entered and closed the door. Both men wore ski masks to hide their faces.

"Take our money and get out!" Barbara's mother screamed as the men tied her up and forced her down on the bed.

"Shut up!" said the bigger man. Barbara watched in panic as he covered her mother's face with a cloth. Her mother began to gasp and fell unconscious.

What do they want?

Barbara held out her hands to allow the man to tie her up. If she didn't put up a struggle, she thought, the two men might not harm her and her mother.

"No," said the bigger man. "We're not tying you up. You're coming with us."

At that moment, Barbara realized what was happening: She was being kidnapped. And she knew, as fear grew in her stomach, that kidnappers often murder their victims—even if the ransom is paid.

Barbara was hustled from the motel and into the back seat of a car. "Chloroform her," the big man ordered.

"No," Barbara cried, panicking. "I'll put my head down. I won't look at you."

With her head down and heart beating wildly with panic, Barbara rode with her two kidnappers for a long time. How long and how far, she wasn't sure. Between the flu and her anxiety, her mind had become a blur.

Barbara's father was a wealthy Miami businessman, which explained why the men had chosen to kidnap her. Barbara knew her father would pay the ransom, no matter how much it was. But the question that she was afraid to ponder was, would she be alive to thank her father after the ransom was paid?

It wasn't until they reached their destination and got out of the car that Barbara realized the second kidnapper wasn't a man at all, but a woman.

"I suppose you know that you are being

kidnapped?" the man asked as they walked out into a wooded area.

"Listen carefully to what I am going to tell you," the man continued. "We are going to put you in an underground room. It is big enough for you to walk around in, but you can only get your air through a battery. The battery will last seven days."

He kept talking, but Barbara was barely listening. "An underground room . . ." The stark reality of her situation suddenly became evident: They were going to bury her alive.

She tried to reason with the two, but it was no use. They refused to listen to her pleas.

The woman had a camera and took Barbara's picture as proof they were the kidnappers.

Then, the kidnappers forced Barbara to go where a large hole in the ground had recently been dug. There were still piles of dirt on the ground next to it. From the amount of dirt visible, Barbara knew the hole was deep.

"I want you to slide down in there," the man said, pressing hard on Barbara's shoulder to push her in.

Terrified at the thought of being buried alive, she struggled to get free. But the man was too strong for her, and in seconds she was forced into the hole and underground "room."

But she found no "room" at the bottom of

the hole. The man had lied to her. It was a box barely large enough for her to sit up in. There was no way to stand or even stretch with any comfort. She was sealed inside a coffin. There was no way she could survive seven days in here. She tried to get up, to get out of the hole before it was too late. "No!" she shouted. "No! Let me out!"

But it was too late. "Here's your water tube," the man said, leaning over the hole. "Behind you is the fan that brings in the air." He mentioned some other things but she couldn't concentrate. Her terror overwhelmed her. "No . . ."

But neither kidnapper listened to her. The man slammed the lid of the box and Barbara was plunged into total darkness.

She heard dirt falling on top of the box, filling up the hole. She was being buried. "No!" she cried into the air vent, "you can't leave me here."

But they did. She continued to call for a long time, or was it only a few minutes? At times like this, time seemed to stand still. Finally the sounds stopped. They were gone. There was only silence, and Barbara was alone in a hole deep underground.

Her sickness worsened by fear, Barbara fell into fitful sleep. She dreamed she was in a coffin and people were piling dirt over her. She awoke with a start and realized it wasn't a dream—it was happening to her.

She was sure her captors wouldn't come

back. They had lied, just as they had lied about the room. There was no reason for them to come back. Whether or not they got their money, they would leave her to die and rot in this box beneath the earth.

What could she do? Nothing. Absolutely nothing. She could cry and scream but no one would hear her in this place out in the woods.

Maybe she should shut off the fan. Stop the air from coming in and just go to sleep— forever.

She wondered about how they would find her—that is, if anyone ever would find her. Someone would find her eventually. But how long would that take, and would there be anything left of her? It might take twenty years to find her corpse. Would worms and other disgusting things have eaten away her flesh and she would be bones? People might never know who she was, who she had been.

For a long time she sobbed softly in the darkness.

Later, she found a switch and turned on the light. There was food and water. At least the man hadn't lied about that. But the sandwiches were already damp from mois- ture and soon would be too moldy to eat.

Barbara knew that a person could stay alive for a long time with very little food. Not that it mattered, however. Her captors had said the air would only last for seven days—

less if she ran down the batteries. She turned off the light.

Barbara imagined herself being blind as she sat in the chilly darkness. When she had been a little girl, she had known a blind person, and she had closed her eyes and wondered what it felt like to be blind. It was scary. She did not want to be blind. She did not want to be in this coffin.

For a little while, she turned the light on again. *Maybe I'll turn it on when I eat,* she thought. Maybe that will be long enough. Then turn it off again. That way, the air will last longer.

She knew that her father would turn heaven and earth to find her. She knew the FBI would be brought in. They would know what to do. Maybe they would find her before it was too late. That was her only hope, and she clung to it.

But as the minutes became hours and the hours became days, Barbara's hopes diminished. She had no sense of how she had been imprisoned; she only knew that her time was running out.

The light didn't work anymore. Perhaps the batteries were weaker than the man had thought. Maybe he had lied about her air, too. Was it running out?

It soon became difficult to breathe, but she wasn't sure if it was just her own anxiety. She had been down there a long time.

Sometimes she got onto her back and

raised her knees. She had long since given up any hope of forcing her way out of the box. There had to be a small mountain of dirt on top of her. If she could open a crack in the box, maybe she could dig her way out. But the box was solid on all four sides. There was no way out.

At first, it was only chilly in the box, but now it was cold—and wet. Barbara's captors had left her a blanket, but it was damp and provided little warmth. She feared her flu would turn into pneumonia.

The food was damp and soggy, and had begun to mold, but she forced herself to eat as much as she could. She knew she had to eat to stay alive.

But why, if no one was going to come for her? If they were coming, they would have been here by now. They weren't coming. She was going to die.

Barbara had been entombed for nearly three and a half days when she heard the sound. It was the rustling of leaves and the crunching of gravel. It sounded like someone was walking on the ground above her.

Was it the kidnappers? Maybe it was just an animal? Whatever it was, she wanted whoever it was to know that she was down there. Frantically, she began to pound on the top of the box, as hard and loud as she could. Then she stopped to listen.

But there was only silence above her. It must have been her imagination. No one was

there. In her damp and hopeless surround-
ings, Barbara began to entertain the thought
that she was losing her mind.

Yet, she couldn't give up. She started to
pound again. Harder and harder, until her
hands ached. Then she stopped . . . and
waited . . . and prayed.

Seconds later, her prayers were answered.
She heard running footsteps, and then a
man's voice shouting, "Barbara! This is the
FBI!"

How long it took for them to dig her out,
she didn't know. What she thought was, did
she look all right? She ran a hand, crusted
with dirt, through her hair. She knew it was
a silly thing to do, but she did it anyway, all
the while wishing they would hurry.

Finally Barbara heard sounds of prying as
her rescuers reached the box and opened
the lid. Suddenly a rush of blinding light
poured into the hole. Barbara blinked and
strained to see as friendly hands reached
down and pulled her from what almost had
become her grave.

"You are the handsomest men I've ever
seen," Barbara told the FBI agents who had
rescued her. The men smiled, and Barbara
could see that their hands bled from digging
the ground. She never would forget these
wonderful men.

Very soon she was reunited with her family. It was the happiest moment of her life.
Her kidnappers were still free, but the FBI

agent who took her home explained that the
agency had several leads and assured her
the captors would soon be captured.

And indeed, it was not long afterward that
the man and woman who had kidnapped
Barbara were captured. They stood trial and
Barbara was called upon to testify. It was
difficult for her to relive those terrible eighty-
three hours she had been buried. Then the
trial was over, and her captors were found
guilty and sent to jail.

With her ordeal finally over, Barbara returned to college and graduated, but the
nightmare she had endured would remain
with her for the rest of her life.

Nightmare on the Haunted Beach

There is an isolated beach at the northwest tip of Scotland called Cape Wrath. The locals believe it is haunted by a strange seafaring man wearing a dark jacket with brass buttons. Some have come upon this sea captain while walking along the mist-shrouded beach at night.

Most eyewitnesses run in the opposite direction upon seeing the ghost's glaring eyes through the fog. One fisherman evidently refused to move out of the captain's path. The fisherman was never seen again, although his cap was found at the edge of the tall cliffs overlooking the turbulent North Sea.

The captain had once lived at a place on the beach called Sandwood Cottage. He had

lived alone and died alone. No one knows
what had caused his death, but it is ru-
mored to have been terrible. There were tales
that three outlaws broke into his home, and
when they were unable to find valuables that
were supposedly hidden there, they took
their wrath out on the captain.

Blood and signs of struggle were apparent
in the cottage, but the captain's body was
never found.

Those responsible were captured but never
stood trial. It is said that while in prison
awaiting judgment, they were visited on a
dark and stormy night. In the morning the
three men mysteriously died. The cause of
their deaths could not be discovered; there
was no mark on any of the bodies. But the
eyes of each were open to reveal that their last
moments were ones of terrible fear.

That was many years ago. Nowadays no
one ventures near the captain's cottage. It
stands on the beach, isolated and forlorn,
battered by the harsh winter seas and
scorched by the hot summer sun. While it
shows signs of age, the cottage still stands,
its wooden beams straight and tall as the
backbone of the strange seafaring man who
once occupied it—and may occupy it still.

It was a chill autumn afternoon in 1962
when two wandering Englishmen on a walking tour came upon Sandwood Cottage. They
had heard tales but discounted them.

"It will be night soon," one of the men,

whose name was Edward, said to the other, Herbert.

Herbert looked at the darkening sky and at the waves breaking over the sand at the edge of the beach. "Aye. And the sea looks angry tonight. I feel we're in for a storm."

Edward pointed toward the cottage. "We can stay there."

"Only if you're not afraid of ghosts," laughed Herbert, who considered himself an educated man, not a believer in ghosts. "I think I'll prefer a ghost to spending the night outside," Herbert answered himself. But the first splash of coming rain on his face convinced him that this was a night to be inside.

And so it was that the two Englishmen camped at Sandwood Cottage on the isolated beach.

The storm came quickly, and they were glad to have shelter from the wind and rain that lashed the cottage. The wooden beams groaned under the fury of the early winter storm, but it was dry inside. And after Edward had managed to build a fire, it was also warm.

"I wonder where those stairs lead to?" Herbert asked, indicating a narrow staircase leading upstairs.

"Probably goes up to a bedroom," Edward replied. "Perhaps there are beds where we can spend the night."

Edward scanned the humble furnishing of the single downstairs room where they stood. There were a table, two wooden chairs, bookcases against the wall, and the fireplace. The furniture was old but functional; the books were worn and weathered from years of neglect.

"No one's lived here for a long time," Herbert muttered. "Still, it's strange that the cottage isn't in more disrepair."

"Perhaps the ghost keeps it up." Edward smiled. He walked to the stairs. "Let's see where these go."

He started up and was halfway to the top when he paused. "What's wrong?" Herbert asked, anxiously.

"Nothing," Edward answered, but the pale look on his face told his friend that this was not true.

Reluctantly, Herbert followed his friend up the steps. He expected them to creak with age, but they did not.

When he stood next to his friend he sensed it—a cold chill that seemed to twist in the pit of his stomach. He felt nauseous and wanted to flee back down the stairs.

Then a hand gripped his shoulder. "No," Edward said. "We've come this far. Let's go the rest of the way."

The cold, uncomfortable clamminess made the last few steps almost painful. But then they were at the top, facing a closed door.

Edward tried to open it, but it would not budge. "It must be locked," said his friend.

"No. But it is stuck. Probably the weather has warped it. Give me a hand."

But, even with both their sets of shoulders pushing against the closed door, it refused to open. All the while, the feeling of something cold surged through Herbert. "Leave it. I want to go downstairs," he said and quickly retreated down the staircase.

"As you will," Edward said, but it was apparent that he too was no longer anxious to see what lay beyond the closed door.

The two men felt better as they sat in front of the fireplace and ate their meager dinner. Outside, the storm continued to howl.

Herbert tried to open one of the books, but its pages came apart in his hand. "No reading tonight," he muttered as he lay down on a blanket near the fire. Edward shook out his blanket and settled down not far from his friend.

How long they slept, neither man knew. But sound awakened them at the same moment. The noise came from the room overhead. Someone was walking across the floor, with heavy footsteps.

"Who?" Herbert asked, fearing the answer.

Edward, saying nothing, quickly got up and walked to the bottom of the stairs. He saw that the door at the top of the stairs was open. Straining his eyes, he could see nothing but blackness within the room.

Edward had started to climb the steps when his friend's hand gripped his arm tightly. "I don't think we should," Herbert said, no longer making any attempt to hide his fear.

"It's either the wind or the ghost," Edward replied. "I want to know which it is."

Suddenly the door slammed shut. And then the downstairs room was plunged into darkness.

The fire had gone out, as if extinguished by a sudden gust of wind. And yet, there was no window open that would allow a wind to enter the cottage. Herbert tried to get the fire going again, but it refused to ignite, almost as if it had a mind of its own.

Edward stepped to the window and listened to the rain. The dark and stormy outdoors provided little illumination. He reached to his pack for matches. A hand gripped his wrist. "Let go," Edward demanded, thinking it was Herbert.

"I'm over here, by the fireplace," Herbert said. And despite the dim gloom, Edward could see that his friend was indeed on the opposite side of the room.

Whatever—or whoever—had gripped Edward's hand was gone. No one was there. Had there ever been someone there or was it his imagination? Edward was shaken and confused.

Dumbfounded, the two men stared at each other when they heard footsteps coming down the steps—heavy, ominous footsteps. They stood side by side for mutual comfort and waited as the footsteps grew louder. Then the sounds stopped, and there was deathly silence.

Suddenly a chair flew across the room, whizzing past their heads, smashing against the wall.

Then, from the bottom of the staircase, they heard a cough. Standing in the gloom was a man dressed in a dark coat, wearing the cap of a sea captain. The man glared at Edward and Herbert with eyes that seemed to blaze with supernatural fire. The two Englishmen experienced a moment of absolute terror, then they slowly started to back away.

But the captain moved toward them, like a ghostly monolith. Suddenly the front door blew open.

"Run!" Herbert yelled. His friend needed no urging. In an instant the two men fled out the door and ran into the full fury of the storm.

Behind them they heard the cottage door slam shut. But the two men ran on in the darkness, afraid to look back, not wanting to know if they were being pursued.

There was one terrible moment as they climbed the rocky path that led up to the bluff. Edward slipped and nearly fell over the side into the sea. But Herbert reached out and pulled him to safety.

Finally exhausted, they spent the rest of the night in the shelter of some rocks above the beach, hoping it was far enough away from the cottage for safety.

After fitful sleep, the two men awoke the next morning to find that the storm had abated. Wet and cold, grateful to be alive, the two men returned to the cottage by daylight. They ventured inside only long enough to retrieve their packs. But it was long enough to notice that the chair that had broken during the night's drama was at the table, all in one piece.

The rest of the day, the two men traveled, trying to get as far from the haunted beach as they could—and vowing never to return.

A Demon Cat
Haunts Washington

Gary Olson, the new guard at the Capitol—where the federal government works in Washington, D.C.—didn't believe the old story. Gary knew one thing for sure: The guard who had told him about the creature that haunted the old tunnels beneath the Capitol was simply spinning a tale to get a rise from the new recruit.

Gary was New York-born and raised and figured that nothing beneath the streets in Washington, D.C., could frighten him—especially not a ghost. At least, not until the night he was alone in the tunnels and saw the demon cat with his own eyes.

Walking through the tunnels was like walking backward in time. While few people came down here anymore, Gary knew these walls held many secrets of historical intrigue. It was easy to believe in ghosts down here in the pale, eerie light in the middle of the night. But, of course, he didn't believe in ghosts. That is, until the fateful night he first encountered the demon cat.

The first time he saw it he wasn't sure what he had seen. A fleeting shadow that vanished into the shadows. It might have been a small animal and that didn't surprise him, although he wondered at the security—or lack of it—that would allow a stray cat to get into the basement.

He *thought* it was cat. A dog would have made more noise. But whatever ran past him was silent, like a cat, he thought.

Probably he would have ignored the creature, but Gary liked animals and the thought of a frightened stray living down here in the tunnels disturbed him. It might be hungry.

The next day, Gary asked the chief guard about the possibility of a stray cat becoming lost in the cavernlike tunnels. Gary was told to forget it—there was nothing down there.

Gary was certain his boss was right, that his imagination had been overactive the night before. But still, he wondered.

Secretly he took a small plate of cat food and left it in a corner where it would not be seen by anyone passing through the tunnel. But three nights later, the food had not been touched, and Gary removed it. And though he looked in all the dark corners with his flashlight, Gary saw no further signs of the evasive animal.

The fourth night was different, however. While making his rounds through basement tunnels of the Capitol, Gary had the eerie sensation that he was not alone. It was midnight and no one had any reason to be down here. Yet he was certain there was someone—or something—lurking nearby.

Then he heard a sound like something scraping against stone. Gary stopped and listened. Only silence. Then it came again. Louder and closer.

It sounded like something scratching against the wall. From inside the wall. Something trapped and trying to get out.

Go down that corridor, Gary thought, and he started to walk down a seldom-used, dark hallway toward the sound's source. This area was very old, and even on the hottest Washington summer days, it was cold down here, and people tended to avoid it. The chill in the air was not quite natural.

Gary slowly walked the hallway, carefully shining his flashlight from side to side. Suddenly the flashlight quit, and he was plunged into darkness.

Irritated, he shook the flashlight back and forth, having just put in new batteries. The only light came from where the hallway branched back into the main corridor from where he had come. He started to walk back that way. Then he stopped.

Behind him he heard footsteps. Not exactly footsteps. More like a soft padding. He whirled around and looked into the blackness, not sure what to expect.

What he saw were the eyes. Two small, slanted yellow eyes stared out of the darkness. And they were moving toward him.

Cautiously Gary began to walk backward, one slow step at a time. As he went, he continued to shake his flashlight in a vain bid to get the light to come back on.

The eyes continued moving toward him, stalking him, like an animal sizing up its prey.

Then Gary took a misstep and momentarily lost his balance, dropping his flashlight to the ground. It clattered sharply, echoing through the darkened hallway. Then, as it rolled over to the wall, its light came on.

Illuminated in a pale glow from the flashlight, Gary saw it. A cat. A huge cat, thin and wiry, with slanted yellow eyes. It was looking at him.

Gary looked at the cat for a long time. Neither he nor the creature moved for what seemed minutes. Something about the animal was not right, but Gary couldn't say what it was.

Suddenly Gary realized that this cat cast no shadow. The light from the flashlight illuminated the cat as it stood by the wall, but the animal had no shadow.

It was the ghost cat, he thought in a rush of fear.

Gary turned and started running toward the main corridor, where he hoped the cat would not follow. But in his haste, he tripped and sprawled onto the hard concrete.

The impact stunned him, and when he momentarily lifted his head from the floor, he found himself staring into the eyes of the ghost cat.

The cat leaned over and licked Gary's face with its sandpaperlike tongue.

Then, as Gary reached out to touch the animal, it leaped over him and ran down the hallway from where it had come.

Retrieving his now-functioning flashlight, Gary walked down the hallway, which came to a dead end at a solid wall. There was no sign of the cat, yet there was no place it could have gone.

When Gary told his boss about the incident the next day, the older man just smiled, knowingly. "You're not the first to have seen it, lad. And you'll not be the last."

Gary admitted to himself that he had been very frightened at first. But this was no longer the case. The cat had not attacked him.

Perhaps it was the food he had left, but Gary knew the cat would not harm him. It might be a ghost cat, but it was certainly no demon, Gary reasoned.

And as he continued to walk basement halls under the Capitol, he sometimes would feel a soft nudge at his leg. He knew the demon cat was accompanying him on his nightly rounds.

The Wolf Man
of Rome

Two thousand years ago in Rome, a man named Niceros was walking with a young soldier who was staying at his home. They were headed for a dinner party some distance away, at a friend of Niceros'.

Niceros did not know the young soldier, but he apparently was on leave and had nowhere to stay in the city. After a chance meeting in the market, Niceros had invited him to be his guest at his hillside villa outside Rome. Niceros lived alone with his servants. Though he was not wealthy, Niceros' house was large—an inheritance from his father.

The soldier was quiet and well behaved. He stayed to himself, walking in the villa's gardens by day and sealing himself in his room to read at night.

When the party invitation came, Niceros thought it might do his guest good to meet others. Strangely reluctant at first, the soldier finally agreed to attend. And so it was that they found themselves walking side by side along the road in the pleasant summer night.

Niceros' friend Trimalchio lived in a very large, secluded villa. Niceros and the soldier would walk through forest and grazing lands where herders tended sheep.

The night air was warm from afternoon heat. Niceros tried to make conversation, but the soldier was not much for small talk. All he would say was that he had come from a northern village and joined the Roman army because it was the one way for a young man without a powerful family to get ahead.

Niceros stopped trying to make conversation and instead looked at the lovely landscape. In the distance, he could hear the bleating of a herd of sheep. Above them, a full moon shone through the tops of trees.

Suddenly Niceros heard something like a growl and turned around sharply. But he was too late, and whatever it was knocked him off his feet. He stumbled and rolled into the grass at the side of the road. Stunned by the impact, he felt something wet licking the back of his head.

Frightened and not knowing what had

happened to the soldier, Niceros did not yell out for him, but lay motionless on the ground. He felt a brush of hair—or thick fur—at the side of his face.

Then there was another growl, and Niceros heard something bounding off. He turned in time to see a huge gray wolf leap off the road and disappear into the forest.

Quickly Niceros was on his feet, still shaking from the encounter. Wolves were not unknown in this area, but one that attacked two men was unheard of. Now he realized that the soldier was missing.

Niceros yelled, but there was no reply. He searched several minutes but could find no trace of the vanished soldier—except for his clothes. They were lying near the side of the road, torn as though by the wolf's claws. Yet there was no trace of blood.

"It makes no sense," Niceros told Trimalchio when he reached the villa. Lanterns illuminated the garden, and several men and women were eating fruit and drinking wine. But Niceros was too shaken to feel like celebrating. And he worried about the young soldier.

"Probably halfway back to his village," Trimalchio said, trying to calm his friend. "You saw no blood, so he was not bitten."

"Perhaps the wolf pursued him."

"Perhaps. But I suspect the wolf is more interested in feasting on sheep than a Roman soldier."

"I can attest to that," a latecomer to the party said. He told of a huge gray wolf that that very evening had attacked a herd of sheep. "The herder came upon the beast and jabbed it in the neck with his pike. The wolf ran off, but it carries a nasty wound."

Niceros remained at the party another hour. Trimalchio offered to have one of his servants accompany his friend home, but Niceros refused. By now the wolf must be long gone from the region.

Still, Niceros kept a brisk pace all the way to his villa. He looked around furtively as he passed through the forest. Once he heard something in the woods. He looked but saw nothing, and began to walk faster.

He was almost running when he reached home.

Niceros started to tell his frightening story to his servant, but before he could speak, the servant beckoned him into the room where the young soldier was staying.

"He returned home without clothes," the servant said. Niceros was only thankful that the man was safe. "He must have been frightened out of his wits."

"He was," the servant replied. "And he was injured."

"Then the wolf did bite him."

The servant shook his head. "It was not a wound from a bite. Perhaps he ran into a sharp branch while running in the woods."

Puzzled, Niceros leaned over the sleeping

soldier. His neck had been bandaged by the servant. Strange, Niceros thought. The man at Trimalchio's house had said the herder gave a neck wound to the wolf who attacked his sheep.

Niceros pulled back the dressing to see a deep wound in the soldier's neck—such as might be caused by a sharp pike.

Niceros retired to his room, but did not sleep well.

In the morning, the young soldier told Niceros that it was time to leave. Though the wound had not healed, the soldier refused to stay.

"It would not be well for you if I did," the soldier said, but would not explain.

After he was gone, the servant called Niceros into the room where the soldier had stayed. "Something I had not noticed the night before."

Niceros looked where the servant pointed. There was blood on the floor, from the soldier's wound. There was something else. It was fur—sheep fur.

"I did not tell you last night," the servant said, "because I was . . . afraid. But the soldier—"

"Tell me what you saw!" Niceros demanded.

"I saw blood on his hands and around his mouth. It was not from his wound, for it was not human blood. It was the blood of a sheep."

Niceros paused and looked past his servant, out through the window, to the road where the soldier had gone. He knew why the soldier could not stay. It would be a full moon tonight—and the soldier once more would be transformed into his other self.

A great gray wolf. A werewolf.

The Ghosts of
Charlton Court

In England in the fifteenth century, two important families hated each other with a vengeance. One of these was the House of Lancaster, whose badge was a red rose, and the other was the House of York, whose badge was a white rose.

The two houses were fierce rivals in their pursuit of power and fought each other for thirty years.

The House of Lancaster obtained the throne of England by an act of Parliament in 1399. In 1422, the House of York declared civil war and the two houses fought for the right to the throne. Finally, after years of battle and tragedies on both sides, Lancaster defeated York and the war ended.

But this is only the beginning of our story,

which picks up with Thornton Rutter in the early 1900's.

Rutter, a direct descendant of the House of York, married a high-bred Sicilian woman and the noble couple had one child, Muriel. A very bright child, Muriel was too sensitive for her own good, some would say, though out of earshot of her father.

While growing up in Charlton Court mansion, Muriel often claimed to hear ghosts in the house. Sometimes she heard tap-tapping on the French doors outside the library. But when she went to peer outside, no one was there.

And sometimes she heard a body dragging itself up the stairs, groaning. Other times she heard a woman screaming. And more than once she thought she saw the woman—a ghostly apparition dressed in historical clothing—rushing upstairs.

When she could not see the ghost, Muriel often "felt" the wind of an apparition passing her on the stairs, and it scared her. Sometimes she saw the woman on the grounds, not screaming but crying. Yet, whenever Muriel tried to approach the woman, she vanished.

At first, Muriel was very frightened by the ghostly images and strange noises. But after a while, she accepted the ghost's presence, and believed that the woman would not harm her or her family. She simply was sad when she saw how upset the ghost appeared to be. She wanted to fix whatever it was that was wrong, but she did not know how.

When Muriel was five or six, her father decided to sell their mansion and move to the seaside village of Rottingdean. The village was adjacent to Brighton on the Channel coast. Muriel was glad and sad; glad to get away from the ghosts that sometimes terrified her, but sad that she could not help the strange, crying woman.

In 1910, a rich American came to buy Charlton Court. To make sure this was the place he wanted to live, he was invited to stay in the house for a weekend. The American first became aware that something was wrong in Charlton Court when he saw two men—dressed in historical costumes of the seventeenth century—dueling with swords on the lawn by the apple orchard. At first, he thought the village was staging some kind of costume party or festival. But, when he approached the two men to talk to them—they vanished!

At this point, Muriel's grandfather felt it only fair to tell the American about the ghosts. Muriel, who was playing nearby, moved closer and listened to the tale her grandfather spun.

"It all began in the years sixteen forty-two to sixteen forty-eight," her grandfather began. "War broke out in England between King Charles and his followers, who were known as the Royalists, or Cavaliers (supporting the throne), and Oliver Cromwell, whose followers were called Roundheads because of their bowllike haircuts."

Muriel listened, and saw that the American was as interested as she was.

"After many battles, Cromwell won the war." Her grandfather paused, and leaned forward toward the American to relate the terrible events. "It was during the war, which lasted about six years, that the young wife of one of my ancestors (who was a Royalist) fell in love with a Roundhead officer.

"The officer came secretly to see her at the house when her husband was away, tapping on the library window with his dagger or sword to attract the wife's attention."

Just like the tapping I heard, Muriel thought, as she moved ever closer, not wanting to miss a single word.

"One day, the husband came home unexpectedly and caught them together. In a jealous rage, he drew his sword and dueled with the Roundhead officer. They fought in the house, and then out through the French doors of the library and in the yard. The husband killed the young officer on the lawn near the apple orchard."

There was silence, then Muriel's grandfather continued. "But the husband, too, was mortally wounded," the grandfather said. "He staggered into the house, dragged his bleeding body up the stairs to his wife's room, and died in her arms in the doorway."

"And those are the ghosts who haunt Charlton Court?" the American asked.

Grandfather nodded. "Their spirits are restless and seek peace, but no one has yet been able to give it to them."

Muriel's grandfather added that he'd seen the two men dueling many times, and had even passed the Roundhead officer on occasion on the driveway. But when her grandfather had tried to approach, the officer had disappeared as though he had never been there.

My grandfather has seen the ghosts too, Muriel thought. *It isn't just my imagination. Charlton Court really is haunted.*

Fascinated by the stories—though he was somewhat intimidated by the ghosts—the American still bought the big mansion.

Muriel and her family moved, and it was not until time passed that she learned what had happened.

Her grandfather told her he had received a letter from the American who bought Charlton Court, and he read it to her. While remodeling the stairway, the American had found a secret room beside the stairs that had been paneled over. Inside he had discovered the skeleton of the Roundhead.

When the American buried the skeleton properly, all the ghost signs ceased. Peace had finally come to the house.

Wave of Death

It all began far from Herbert Nishimoto's home on the island of Hawaii—on the ocean floor off the coast of Alaska. Before it was over, it would become the most terrifying day of the teenager's life.

But for the moment, Herbert was asleep and was unaware of the undersea earthquake raging thousands of feet below the surface, on the northern slope of the Aleutian Trench.

It was 2 A.M., and the men assigned to night watch at the Coast Guard lighthouse on Unimak Island were bored. Suddenly the building began to shake. They knew it was an earthquake—a big one! They sought shelter in the doorway or under tables.

Then the shaking stopped, the earth

settled, and the danger was over—or so they thought.

Twenty minutes later, giant waves, over a hundred feet high, crashed over Unimak Island and washed the lighthouse and Coast Guardsmen into the sea. There were no survivors that fateful morning of April 1, 1946—April Fools' Day.

Five hours later, in the town of Ninole on the southwest coast of the big island of Hawaii, fourteen-year-old Herbert Nishimoto had no idea what had happened two thousand miles away—but he was about to find out.

Herbert had spent the weekend with a friend. They had had a good time the evening before, and this morning Herbert awoke to another fine Hawaiian day.

Suddenly there were shouts outside. Herbert ran to the door and saw his friend Daniel Akiona running down the road, shouting, "Tidal wave!"

Herbert saw huge waves coming from the sea and smashing against the boat ramp. "Quick!" Daniel urged, pointing toward his house, which was opposite the boat ramp. "We'll be safe in my house."

The two boys ran as fast as they could, terrified of being caught by the monstrous waves and washed into the ocean.

But as they reached what they hoped would be shelter, a giant wave crashed upon them and shattered the house like a toy stomped by a giant's foot.

Then, his worst fear became a reality. Herbert was swept up by the wave, lifted to a dizzying height, then tossed down into the water and sucked out into the ocean. He was going to die.

But luck was with him that morning, for the giant wave deposited him near the reef that protected the bay. He gasped for breath as his head broke the surface. Not far away, he saw someone clinging to a log, but there was no sign of his friend.

As the next wave came, Herbert tried to get out of his tight jeans so that he could swim. But he had only one leg free as the wave hit, and the loose leg of his jeans caught on the reef. Herbert struggled but was battered against the rocks by the fury of the sea.

Finally, his breath almost gone, he tore free of his jeans and swam to the surface. He found himself floating in a caldron of debris—broken pieces of houses and boats. But he was alive.

Then he saw that he was surrounded by sharks that had been forced into the bay by the waves. Had he survived one disaster, only to be lost to another?

Fortunately the sharks seemed as bewildered as he, and Herbert had a chance to escape. Just ahead of him was the floor of someone's cottage. Swimming with his remaining energy, Herbert reached the safety of this makeshift raft and pulled himself aboard.

As he lay stunned, he saw the town of Ninole and the boat ramp. But most of the boats were gone—victims of the tsunami. The killer wave from Alaska had turned April Fools' Day 1946 into a day of death and destruction the islands would long remember and Herbert Nishimoto could never forget.

The Ghost and the Movie Star

We expect to find haunted houses at ends of lonely roads in secluded areas, or to be old, Victorian-style mansions in shadowy parts of town. But any house can be haunted—even in Beverly Hills.

In summer 1964, Elke Sommer—who had recently been in films with Paul Newman and Peter Sellers—and her reporter husband, Joe Hyams, bought an elegant two-story house in a quiet area of Beverly Hills.

For a few days, nothing unusual happened, and the couple was delighted with the new home.

On the fourth day, Elke invited a journalist to join her for afternoon tea. Elke was in the house, and the woman guest was sitting near the pool when she noticed something—or, rather, someone.

She saw a middle-aged man, in a black suit with a white shirt and tie, emerge from the shadows and walk quickly around the pool. He seemed intent on something, and apparently did not notice her. The guest assumed that he was visiting Elke's husband, though she remembered that Hyams was not home.

Turning to introduce herself, the guest was shocked to see that he had vanished. She had only looked away for a moment; how could he have gone so quickly?

Elke was stunned when her guest told her what had happened—no one else was in the house. Perhaps he was a neighbor, but where had he come from—and where had he gone?

The incident was forgotten until two weeks later. The worker who had come to clean the swimming pool was startled to see a man in a black suit, walking with his hands behind his back toward the house and enter the dining room.

Realizing the man should not be there, the worker quickly crossed to the dining room window and looked inside. The man had vanished.

After that, Elke and her husband began noticing that something definitely was strange about this new house.

Noises awakened them in the middle of the night. Loud noises from the dining room sounded like drawers being opened and furniture moved.

Fearing they were being burglarized, Hyams rushed downstairs to confront the intruder—before he realized that such bravado was probably not a good idea. But when he entered, no one was in the room, and all the furniture was in its proper place.

The following month, Hyams was alone in the house while his wife was away. But he had a feeling that he was not alone, that something was in the house with him.

Each morning, he discovered the same bedroom window wide open, even though he had locked it the night before. Yet there was no sign that anyone had entered or left.

With growing apprehension and curiosity, Hyams purchased three miniature radio transmitters, and placed them so that they would turn on when activated by a noise. They would broadcast sounds to three radios in the upstairs bedroom, to be recorded on three tape recorders in an elaborate trap to catch the mysterious intruder.

Now the sound of chairs being moved came through the radio, and Hyams hurried downstairs. This time, he carried a pistol.

But when he entered the dining room, the sounds ceased—and all the furniture was exactly where it had been left.

The sounds were captured on the tape recorder, so it had not been his imagination.

Someone—or something—had been in the dining room.

Later, a friend stayed at the house while the Hyamses were away. The friend heard the sounds, but could not find anyone in the house.

Even a private detective hired by Hyams to watch the house when the Hyamses were gone could not find an intruder. But he did report that lights would go on and off all at once when no one was home. Other visitors saw the same man moving about the house.

They finally invited psychics to determine if a ghost was haunting their home. Several psychics reported seeing the man. Hyams thought the ghost might be a doctor that he had worked with who had died recently. Elke thought he might be the ghost of her father.

One psychic told them that they would move within two years, and that until then they might be in danger. She foresaw a possible fire in the very near future.

But it was a lovely house, and the Hyamses were not anxious to move. They were, however, a bit frightened by the ghost. And the psychic's warning of a fire made things even scarier.

It was raining that March night when the Hyamses went to bed. In the middle of the night they were awakened by loud pounding on the bedroom door.

Hyams awoke from deep sleep and rushed to the door, throwing it open. No one was there—but the hallway was filled with smoke. The house was on fire!

Luckily, the Hyamses managed to crawl out the window and scramble to safety. The next morning, after firemen had put out the fire, the battalion chief led them to where the fire had started—the mysterious dining room.

This was enough. The Hyamses put the house up for sale and moved out. They were thankful to leave the ghost who had disturbed their sleep. But they were grateful for the strange pounding on the door. The ghost who had given them many sleepless nights had probably also saved their lives.

Fire Storm

November 1994 was the hottest month thirteen-year-old Mike Caruso could remember this late in the year. As he and his friend Sean got off the school bus at Carbon Canyon Road, in Malibu, California, Mike felt the bone-dry wind gusting down from the canyon and smelled fragrant tinder-dry sagebrush.

Everyone thinks of Malibu as a glamorous beach town, filled with luxurious oceanfront homes of movie stars. But a large part of Malibu is inland, in the foothills of the Santa Monica Mountains. Many homes there are also working ranches. Mike's parents had such a ranch.

Sean Rikkard, a thirteen-year-old red-haired boy with freckles, was spending the week visiting Mike while his parents were in New York on a business trip. He and Mike had been friends since the third grade, but since Sean had moved nearby to Santa Monica, they didn't get to see as much of one another. Mike was as dark as Sean was fair, and as quiet as Sean was boisterous.

"Let's ride Julie and Blaze up to Saddle Peak," Sean suggested as they trudged down the dusty road that led to the Caruso Ranch. Julie and Blaze were two mares that the Carusos had raised since birth. They were gentle as lambs, and even Emma Caruso (whom her son called a "professional worrier") wasn't nervous when the boys were out with them.

"You know what my mom's gonna say," Mike said as they entered the kitchen.

"Yeah," Sean said. "Do your homework first." He stepped to the refrigerator to get something cold to drink, and saw a paste-it note stuck to the door.

Dear Mike, the note read. *I've gone to pick up your father at work while the other car is in the shop. Be back by dinner. Don't pig out on snacks! Love Mom.*

"We're in luck!" Sean cried. "Let's go!" The boys tossed their bookbags onto the kitchen counter, then ran out the back door to the stable.

Julie and Blaze were the only "resident" horses. Mr. Caruso was a lawyer, but had cut his hours to spend more time doing what he loved: breeding horses. Arabian and Appaloosas were his favorite breeds. And there were three Arabian mares and a yearling Appaloosa stallion in the stucco-covered stable.

Sean lifted the latch on the stable's wooden door. Mike, behind him, gazed past the line of eucalyptus trees on the dirt road leading into the hills. A gray-brown cloud drifted above the hills. *Was it dust?* Mike wondered. He sniffed the air.

"Do you smell something weird?" Mike asked Sean as they headed into the dim coolness of the stable.

"Only your breath," Sean said, laughing in reply.

Once inside the stables, Mike noticed that the horses were restless. Even normally placid Julie whinnied and snorted. Sean didn't notice, and Mike shrugged as he saddled Blaze.

The boys rode out of the yard and onto the track leading into the hills and the gravest danger of their young lives. It was on that hot, dry day in November—with the arid Santa Ana winds blowing to the ocean from the deserts—that the deadly Malibu Fire struck.

Sean, taking the lead on Blaze, saw it first. "Look!" He pointed as they reached the crest of the hill. Below was the leading edge of the fire—a mile-long swath of destruction—burning trees, brush, and the bone-dry grass that covered the Santa Monica Mountains.

Blaze and Julie whinnied nervously and pawed the ground.

"We'd better head back," Mike said worriedly, as the boys heard the distant wail of approaching sirens.

Sean stared in fascination at the blaze. "Let's go down and get a better look," he suggested. "I want to watch those firefighters work."

A road wound in from nearby Pacific Coast Highway, and both boys could see sun glinting off nearby fire trucks.

Mike was concerned. Two years before, his dad had helped neighbors battle a small brush fire that almost got out of control. He'd seen damage even a little fire could do. The neighbor had lost his outbuildings and an old horse; a family pet had panicked and dashed into the flames to his death.

"No! We head back now!" Mike said.

But Sean ignored his friend and turned Blaze down the hill. Before Mike could react, Sean was a hundred yards away. "Come back!" Mike called.

Down the hill, Sean could feel waves of heat blow toward him on the gusty winds that roared up the hill. Now he could see the fire engines heading his way. *This is gonna be neat,* he thought.

But suddenly a random gust of wind whipped flaming cinders from the burning brush across the road. Blaze—already spooked by the fire—suddenly reared up on her hind legs and pawed the air as if to fight flames with her forelegs.

Sean was tossed off the horse's back and fell to the ground. Sean was hurt! As Mike wheeled Julie to head down, he saw Blaze turn and gallop uphill. She wanted no more of this fire.

Mike leapt off Julie before the horse had stopped and ran to Sean, who was sitting up and rubbing his head. "Ow. That hurt," he said. Mike helped his friend to his feet, while watching the front line of the fire draw nearer. "Come on, Sean! We've got to get out of here!" Both boys coughed as the clouds of searing smoke rolled over them.

Mike helped still-groggy Sean onto Julie, then climbed on in front of him. "Hang on to me," he told Sean over his shoulder. Behind, he saw the fire trucks pulling up. A yellow-helmeted fireman called out, but Mike couldn't hear him. He urged Julie to go faster.

Back at the ranch, Blaze was nibbling grass in the field next to the stables, still nervous and uneasy. Mike and Sean hopped off Julie, tied both horses, then ran into the house. "We've got to call Mom and Dad," Mike said. "That fire's coming this way!"

But when Mike dialed the phone, he got a strange noise and recorded voice: "All circuits are busy. Please try again later." The lines were jammed with thousands of frantic callers trying to find out about the fire, which had already burned almost six thousand acres and destroyed fifty homes.

Down on the Pacific Coast Highway—the only safe way out of the area—the situation was grim. Emma and Rudy, Mike's parents, were stuck in a crazed traffic jam. There were frantic Malibu residents hurrying to see what had happened to their houses and fire trucks and other emergency vehicles. Rudy tried the mobile phone in the car, but got the same "circuits busy" message that Mike had heard.

Back at the Caruso ranch, the boys watched in growing anxiety as the first orange tendrils of flame appeared on the crest of the hill behind the property. And then, in a truly terrifying instant, saw flames rise up on the other side, coming at them from the road. The boys were surrounded!

In the stable, the horses whinnied and kicked at their stalls, smelling the smoke. "We've gotta get outta here. And we've got to take the horses with us!" Mike cried.

"But how?" Sean asked. "You saw how Blaze was. They'll go crazy when they get near the fire."

"We've got to try. We can't just leave them here," Mike replied.

Mike ran to the stable, followed by Sean. By now a huge plume of smoke covered the sky, turning day into eerie twilight darkness.

Inside the stable, Mike went from stall to stall, petting the frightened horses, trying to calm them. Only the yearling was too young to be afraid.

Mike grabbed a tangled clump of leather straps and metal from the wall and tossed it to Sean. "Put these on the horses. We'll lead 'em out."

"What are you gonna do?" Sean asked.

"Get blindfolds for them." Mike remembered reading somewhere that if a horse couldn't see a fire, he wouldn't be as skittish and hard to handle.

Mike and Sean led the horses, all blindfolded except for Julie, out of the stable. Though they couldn't see the flames—now almost surrounding the ranch property—the horses were still frightened. Cinnabar, the youngest mare, yanked her head back, pulling the reins out of Sean's hand. Mike grabbed them in time, or the horse would have bolted. The flames drew nearer.

On the jammed Pacific Coast Highway, Rudy had taken the wheel of the Land Rover. A few hundred yards up the highway, Rudy and his wife could see Carbon Canyon Road . . . but traffic was not moving. Panicked drivers honked their horns futilely. Smoke drifted down to the highway from the fire. Sirens sounded off in the distance. It was a scene from someone's nightmare.

Finally Rudy turned to Emma: "Hang on!" He cranked the wheel and stepped on the gas. The Land Rover bounced into the ditch and up onto the other side of the hill.

Heedless of honking horns and shouts from the police, Rudy drove across the grassy sward at the side of the road, hitting a mailbox and a For Sale sign, before reaching the Carbon Canyon turnoff. He swung around a Highway Patrol officer who was directing traffic away from the turnoff, and sped up the road.

In the canyon where the Caruso ranch sat, the first flames licked at the wooden rails and posts of the corral. On the road leading from the ranch, Mike and Sean battled frightened horses and ever-thickening smoke. They coughed continuously, and Sean realized he should have soaked cloths for them to use to breath through.

Burning embers drifted from above. *What will we do if that brush ahead of us catches fire?* Mike wondered. The fire crept up behind them, whipped by high winds.

Sean dropped to his knees, racked with coughing. "I can't. I can't do this," he gasped.

"You've got to!" Mike urged, grabbing Sean by the arm and—coughing himself—taking the reins of all six horses. Mike, his eyes and lungs burning, tied the reins together, and then helped Sean onto Julie's back.

The two boys headed down the road. Mike could see the brush smoldering on either side of them, and could feel the heat from the second fire.

The fire was almost upon the boys when they heard a noise from ahead and saw a light through the smoke. The Carusos' Range Rover roared around a bend, skidding on gravel and skewing around 180 degrees, as Rudy cranked the wheel and hit the brakes to avoid hitting the boys and the horses.

"Mike! Sean! Thank God!" Emma exclaimed as she and Rudy dashed from the car to the boys.

Mike coughed as he hugged his parents. "We didn't . . . want to leave . . . the horses," Mike told them between racking coughs.

Glancing at the flames behind them, Rudy quickly tied the horses' reins to the rear of the Range Rover as Emma helped the two boys into the backseat. Taking the wheel, Rudy drove as fast as he could back down the mountain road, the high winds whipping the flames behind him into a frenzy.

At the bottom of the hill, they almost had an accident when several fire trucks wheeled up the rutted path toward them. "They'll soon have the fire under control," Rudy said as the trucks went past them up the hill.

When they reached the highway, Rudy pulled over and saw the exhausted boys. "We may lose our house," he told them. "But we can rebuild that. What we couldn't replace is what the two of you saved." He looked at the horses—weary and still frightened, but safe.

The Malibu fire of 1994 was the worst in almost forty years, and destroyed more than twenty thousand acres and 125 homes. The corral and two outbuildings at the Caruso ranch burned, but the fire spared the house and stable. Most important, after being treated for smoke inhalation and exhaustion, Sean and Mike had survived their brush with fiery death.

The Scariest Place on Earth

Someone once said that the scariest place on earth is directly in the path of an onrushing hurricane. "Above the howling wind and the driving rain, the villagers of Manpura Island could hear an unholy roar welling up from the Bay of Bengal." *Time* magazine thus reported the story of a deadly hurricane that killed more than half a million people in India in 1970.

Donna thought she knew all about hurricanes. She had read about them in school and had experienced fierce storms growing up in South Florida. But she was not prepared for Hurricane Andrew as it moved relentlessly across the Caribbean, toward her home.

On television she followed Andrew's path as it hit the Florida coast and came toward her home. Already thousands of people had been evacuated. But her father felt their home, only a few years old, was sturdy enough to withstand Andrew's savage winds, and they had not fled.

Donna's mother was frightened and thought that, perhaps, they should leave, but Donna and her little brother wanted to stay. They foresaw a great adventure.

On television Donna could see deserted downtown Miami Beach. No cars were in the street, and the people who had not gone huddled in doorways and inside buildings. If they weren't afraid, then she wouldn't be.

Donna's father went outside one last time to check that everything was okay. The windows were boarded up, the cracks all sealed. "Tomorrow morning it will be all over," he said, smiling at her when he came inside.

Donna and her brother went to sleep in beds that her mother had made in the down-stairs playroom. She didn't want them to be alone upstairs. As the howling wind began, Donna was glad not to be in her second-story bedroom.

It grew late and the wind became louder. They heard objects thrown about outside. Something sounded like an awful scream.

Her father said it was only a tree being uprooted.

Then, sometime after midnight, the power went out. With windows sealed, it became pitch-black inside the house. Outside, the wind was screaming louder and louder. Donna and her brother huddled together. *This is no longer an adventure*, she thought. *This is really scary.*

All through the night there was a terrible battering against the house. Donna could hear the glass in one window shatter as something smashed against it, but the boards held fast and the storm didn't penetrate the house.

Just before dawn there was a terrible shaking and Donna feared that the house would be lifted from its foundation and carried off. She had read about such things happening, and now she was afraid it was going to happen to her.

She wanted to scream, but her little brother was very frightened so she tried to look braver than she felt as she put her arms around him. "It's going to be all right," she said, though she didn't believe it.

"We should have left," her mother said.

Donna's father didn't reply; he was no longer quite so certain that the house would stand up against the terrible storm. He hadn't expected it to be as bad as this.

Then the rain came. It sounded like machine-gun fire as drops splashed the house. It seemed to last forever, threatening to wash the house away.

But then, as morning finally came, the wind ceased to howl like the roar of an angry dragon and the rain softened into drizzle.

"It's over," her father told them as they listened to the transistor radio. "The hurricane moved faster than anyone expected. Otherwise we might not have been so lucky." He looked at his family huddled together in the playroom, their faces illuminated by the pale glow of several flashlights.

Later that morning, when the hurricane had passed, Donna went outside with her father. Their neighborhood looked as if it had been bombed. All the trees were uprooted and lying about like matchsticks. Their house was damaged but standing; other homes had not been so lucky. Trees had crashed through the roofs, and other houses had windows broken and whole walls ripped off.

Neighbors who had stayed, like Donna's family, now came out. Donna saw them standing in little circles or walking about, because no car could drive with fallen trees and debris clogging the streets. Everyone seemed dazed by what the hurricane had done. Some people were hurt, but no one had been killed. There was something to be thankful for.

"The next hurricane that comes," Donna said to her father, "let's go away."

He looked down at her and nodded. No one wanted to be in the scariest place on earth. Not if he or she had a choice.

Attack of the Sasquatch

Because of heavy snows, it was May before Ray Tollefson and Jim Hunt could return to their mining claim in Ape Canyon, near Mount Saint Helens in Washington. They were eager to begin looking for gold Ray felt sure was there. The year was 1924, and memories of the 1898 Yukon strike—where twenty-two million dollars in gold was mined in a single year—were fresh in their minds.

The previous year, Ray and two other miners had come across several nuggets as they panned along Ape Creek. The approach of winter made further exploration impossible, and the miners had to file a claim with the state before they could do any further mining.

Even in 1924, hundreds of dollars in tools and equipment, and the filing of paperwork were required to stake a claim. So Ray agreed to go in with the others as partners. If they found gold, they'd all be rich. If not, they'd move on.

Ray and Jim were on their way to meet the Linden brothers, the other two miners who shared in the claim. Together, they would make the day-long trip to the claim site on top of mules loaded down with supplies.

As Ray and Jim arrived at their meeting place—a saddle between two mountains in the pine woods of the southern Cascade Range—Jim saw them first. "There they are," he said, pointing.

Tom and George Linden had driven inland from Kelso in their Model T Ford, while Ray and Jim had brought the mules and supplies from the south, across the Lewis River.

"Thought you fellas would never get here," Tom joked as the four men shook hands.

"If we'd had a Tin Lizzy like you instead of these mules, we'd 'a beat you here," said Ray with a grin.

The four men unloaded the rest of the supplies (including dynamite and canned goods from the Model T), and put them on the mules. Then they headed toward their claim.

Arriving by mid-afternoon at the cabin they had built the year before, they stored their supplies and quickly went to work. The first task was building a mall dam and sluice box on the creek. Jim hobbled the two mules near the creek, making sure they had plenty of grass for grazing.

Ray was the first to see them. Hot and sweaty from hard work, he went upstream a few yards to get a drink and wash his face in the glacially cold water. As he bent over the stream, he saw movement out of the corner of his eye. Ray whirled and looked into the woods. *Something* moved among the trees.

"Is that you, Jim?" Ray called. There was no answer. Nothing moved. After a moment, Ray shrugged. *Must have been a deer,* he thought.

Later, Tom built a fire and the men cooked dinner. Ray glanced into the woods uneasily. Something about the mysterious figure he'd seen bothered him. He realized it couldn't have been a deer. It was taller, almost like a man.

Not sure what he was looking at, Ray moved closer. Suddenly a pair of glowing eyes stared out from the woods! Ray yelled, "Hey!" The others turned to look—and jumped to their feet. A huge, lumbering shape—almost seven feet tall—vanished behind a tree.

"What was that?" Tom stared into the woods, slack-jawed.

"An Indian . . . maybe an Indian," George said, not believing his own words.

Jim got to his feet. "Not a chance. But the Indians around here have stories about some big, hairy creature. They call it Sasquatch," he said.

Ray reported what he'd seen. "I thought I was seeing things," he ended. "I guess not."

The four hurriedly put out the fire and headed into their cabin. Tom stoked the wood stove while Ray lit the kerosene lamps. Suddenly the night seemed mysterious, menacing.

As if by agreement, the men didn't talk about the mysterious figure. It was almost as if the whole thing had never happened. Later, they unfolded iron cots they'd brought and went to bed.

Thump! George awakened with a start. Something had hit the wall next to his bed. He sat up and peered out the tiny window. It was pitch-black.

Thump! This time, Jim awoke. "What was that?" he asked.

Now all four were awake. As Ray lit the lantern, the men heard another thump! This one was on the roof . . . almost as if something—or someone—had landed on it.

"It's that thing in the woods!" Tom said, breathless. A series of thumps, accompanied by an unearthly screech, echoed through the tiny cabin.

"There's more of them!" Ray shouted. They all gazed as another shaggy form appeared

at the window, silhouetted in dim starlight.
The four men yelled in fright.

There was a terrifying braying noise from
outside. "They're after the mules!" Ray
shouted.

Now the window shattered as a huge,
hairy fist smashed the glass. More screeches
and inhuman roars echoed through the forest. The cabin was besieged by terrifying,
monstrous creatures. Inside, Jim, Ray, and
the Linden brothers huddled in fear.

The attack seemed to taper off. But still,
the four men—taking quick, frightened
glances out the shattered window—could see
several large, furry shapes just outside. An
occasional screech made the men jump.

"We've gotta get outta here!" Tom said,
crouching near the door.

"I'm not goin' out there!" his brother
George replied.

The rest of that seemingly endless night,
the four men stayed alert, terrified of more
attacks from the mysterious creatures.
"They're Sasquatch," Jim said, and no one
doubted him.

At the first light of day, Ray cautiously
opened the door and looked out at the forest.
The strange creatures were nowhere in
sight.

Cautiously, the four men went outside.
The mules had vanished. Whether they'd
run off—or something far worse had happened—the men never learned.

And they didn't stick around to find out. George, Tom, Ray, and Jim grabbed whatever they could carry and left Ape Creek as fast as their feet would carry them. If gold was to be found here, they were willing to leave it to the Sasquatch!

Terror at the Circus

The circus was in town. For Kristy and Paul Lawson, that meant an exciting day of clowns, wild animals, cotton candy—and, if their mom, Karen, would allow it—a ride on an elephant.

The Southwest Circus visited Albuquerque, New Mexico, every June. Since Kristy and Paul had been old enough to go to the circus, they'd wanted to ride Juliet, an aging elephant that the circus equipped with baskets on her sides to carry children around the sawdust center ring between shows.

"Please, Mom, can we go?" Kristy pleaded as the Lawsons entered the big top.

"You said we could when we were older," Paul added. "Now we're older."

Karen relented when she saw Juliet calmly

carrying a pair of children around the ring. The elephant's trainer, Tim Reilly, watched over her to make sure no one accidentally fell off.

"All right," she told Paul and Kristy. "But just a short ride."

Eagerly, Paul and Kristy climbed into the baskets on either side of the elephant. Reilly nudged Juliet with a stick and the giant animal began lumbering forward.

Then, for no apparent reason, Juliet went berserk. With a roaring trumpet, she stepped out of the ring, knocked over her trainer, and smashed through the tent entrance.

Outside, terrified spectators scattered to get out of the path of the rampaging elephant. Fearfully, Karen Lawson ran outside after her children, who were screaming atop Juliet's back. The baskets bounced alarmingly.

Karen watched in horror as Paul, her youngest, bounced out of the basket and to the ground. The elephant's rear foot just missed crushing him. A spectator ran over, picked Paul up, and carried him out of harm's way.

Reilly hurried onto the scene aboard Clyde, another elephant, to try to calm Juliet. But the maddened beast ignored the other elephant. Kristy was alone and terrified.

By now, Albuquerque policeman Dwayne Peters had arrived. He bravely ran in front of

Juliet, and tried to distract her so others could rescue Kristy. But the rogue elephant grabbed him with her trunk and hurled him violently to the ground.

Stunned, Peters saw the huge beast rampaging above him. He rolled out of the way, but the elephant's foot came down on his leg, breaking it in several places.

Reilly brought Clyde alongside Juliet and managed to grab Kristy out of the basket a moment before the maddened elephant crushed the basket against a light pole.

Surrounded by circus workers, Juliet turned, trumpeting. Just then, Peters raised his pistol and fired at the beast. But the small-caliber bullet had no effect. Instead, Juliet turned and headed back to the injured policeman, ready to crush him.

At the very last moment, another police officer fired a high-powered rifle that finally brought down the huge beast. Only three steps away from the downed policeman, Juliet crumpled into a heap.

Kristy and Paul were bruised and frightened but none the worse for wear. Still, it would be a long time before either of them felt the same about going to the circus.

Strange Warning

In 1954, Bill Collins got a warning that saved his and his family's lives. The Collins family—Bill and Ellen, and their sons, Jeff and Peter—lived in the small town of Murrell's Inlet, south of Myrtle Beach, South Carolina, in a whitewashed, tin-roofed cottage. Bill was a skilled finish carpenter, whose work sometimes took him away from his family for days—often weeks—at a time.

It was early October. Bill was heading to Savannah, Georgia, to work on a remodel job. His specialty was restoration of old houses, and the Savannah area had plenty of Civil War–era homes that needed work.

"I'll be back by Friday evening, honey," he said that Tuesday, before the sun was up, as he kissed his wife good-bye.

"There's a hurricane in Haiti that might be headed this way," said Ellen, worried.

"The weatherman said it's due to hit Florida, not here. And not Savannah, either," Bill said reassuringly, as he climbed into his battered Ford pickup. "Kiss the kids for me."

Waving, Bill cranked the engine, put the truck in gear, and headed off.

The day dawned clear and bright as Bill made the three-hour drive to Savannah. *That hurricane'll probably blow off over the ocean and never get this far,* Bill thought as he squinted into the bright sun.

Arriving in Savannah, Bill checked in with the foreman and got to work. The suburban Savannah mansion, dating from Colonial times, was being restored as an historical monument by the city and state governments. As a result, Bill spent a lot of time in consultations on the right style of wood-carving for this stair rail, or the historically accurate molding for that doorjamb.

That Tuesday afternoon, while Bill was talking with another worker, he had the strangest feeling that someone was watching him. He turned—and there, standing on the sidewalk, was a tall, thin man, dressed all in gray, looking at him.

At that instant, a car went by on the street behind the man. The afternoon sun, reflecting off the car's window, blinded Bill for an instant. When his sight returned, the man was gone!

Bill asked his coworker, "Did you see that man?"

"What man?" was the response. Bill shook his head. Maybe he'd imagined it.

In October 1954, a tropical storm began in the "storm trough" of the south Atlantic. Building speed, it headed for Haiti. By the time the storm had enough force to be termed a hurricane and the National Weather Service named it Hazel, it had increased to winds of more than 110 miles per hour, across a front of thirty miles. Haiti, warned by radio, prepared for the storm.

Bill Collins finished work for the day and headed back to the room he'd rented earlier. He planned to shower, grab a quick meal, and go to bed. The long drive from Murrell's Inlet and the day's work had tired him.

Heading for a nearby coffee shop, Bill rounded the corner of the street. There, standing in the middle of the road, was the man in gray! Bill was stunned. He looked away then back again . . . once more, the man had disappeared. Bill forgot about his dinner and headed back to his room in a daze. He called Ellen that evening, but didn't tell her what he'd seen. *She'd think I'm crazy,* he thought. He began to wonder if he was.

Hurricane Hazel hit Haiti with incredible force. Trees were uprooted, houses and cars—even buses—tossed about like child's toys, whole villages flattened. When its force had passed, three hundred people had been killed.

In Savannah the next morning, clouds rolled in and the sky turned leaden gray. Bill glanced up as he headed for his job site.

It looked like a big storm was coming. But the morning weather report on his truck radio had said that Hurricane Hazel would make landfall in the United States somewhere in northern Florida.

At the old mansion, workmen were putting tarpaulins on the unroofed sections of the house, preparing for rain. Bill considered himself fortunate: He was working on the lower floors, in a still-roofed portion of the old structure, away from any rain that might blow in.

Bill carried his tool bags into the entry hall of the mansion, which faced a porte cochere over a long drive. Glancing out the window at the rain—now beating down steadily—he set to work pulling off the molding from around a window. Across the entry, Hank, a sandy-haired carpenter, measured stock for the new moldings.

Bill held his carpenter's rule up to the window. As he did, he happened to look out the window into the drive.

There stood the man in gray!

Bill let out a yell. "Hey!" Then he ran out the door. Bounding down the steps of the porte cochere two at a time, Bill landed in the muddy drive. The man in gray had disappeared. Bill looked frantically up and down the drive. He caught a glimpse of something at the head of the driveway, at the street. Bill called again: "Wait!"

Bill ran up the drive, heedless of the pouring rain. As he reached the curb, he dimly saw the man in gray, pointing. "What is it? What do you want?" Bill called out. But the rain came down harder and the man in gray vanished like a wisp of smoke.

Hank, the other carpenter, came up the drive and joined Bill. "What's going on?" he asked, grinning. "You took off like you'd seen somebody who owed you money."

"Don't tell me you didn't see that fellow standing in the drive a minute ago," Bill said.

Hank shook his head. "I turned when I heard you yell and saw you take off," Hank replied. "I didn't see anybody else." He turned to go back in. "Come on. We're standing out in the rain like a couple of fools."

But Bill shook his head. "That man . . . whatever he was . . . was trying to tell me something."

"Let me know when you figure it out," Hank said, hurrying back toward the house. "I'm getting out of this rain."

Bill stared up the street, not hearing Hank. *What had the man in gray been pointing at?* By now soaked to the skin—but ignoring it—Bill walked up the suburban street a few paces to a corner where he'd seen the man disappear. There was a highway sign, with various destinations and mileage to them: Hilton Head, Charleston, Myrtle Beach.

It hit Bill like a bolt of lightning: The man in gray had been telling him to get back to his family, to go home! Bill dashed back to the job site, gathered his tools, and, telling the foreman that an emergency had come up, hopped into his truck and drove off.

Weather reports aren't always accurate. Changes in water temperature in the North Atlantic, a dust storm in Northern Africa, all can make man's forecasts about the weather seem as reliable as predictions on a horse race. Hurricane Hazel, up to now tracing its deadly path north and west from Haiti, suddenly changed course and headed north. There were no weather satellites in 1954, so this fact went undetected for six hours. At last, the Chinese crew of a freighter, heading north from Panama to New York, radioed a frantic SOS: Their ship had been struck by Hurricane Hazel, and was sinking in the waters due east of the Georgia coast.

The Coast Guard sent out a cutter. But the freighter *Star of Malaya* had sunk with all hands. Six more hours would pass before the weather stations reported the hurricane's change in direction. But that was several hours *after* the man in gray had last appeared to Bill Collins.

Bill drove as fast as he dared over the rain-slick highway north to Charleston, then toward Murrell's Inlet. Frantic with worry, he turned on the radio, only to hear that predictions for Hurricane Hazel still had her making landfall in northern Florida.

I must be crazy, Bill thought. But he remembered how the man in gray had been pointing . . . pointing north . . . pointing to where his family was . . . Bill peered through the driving rain, as the windshield wipers tried to keep up with the downpour.

It was over two hundred miles to Murrell's Inlet. The winds had picked up, rocking Bill's pickup, and threatening to hurl it sideways on the slick highway.

It was evening as Bill pulled into the graveled driveway of his house. He dashed up the walkway, arriving at the door just as Ellen opened it to see who had come.

"Bill! What's the matter? Did something happen at work?" she asked.

"I'm fine. But we've got to get out of here," Bill replied as he hugged her quickly and entered the house.

Jeff and Peter, the children, were in pajamas listening to the radio as their father hurried in. Seeing their startled expressions, Bill smiled. "Hi, guys," he said. "We've got a surprise for you. We're going on an adventure."

Jeff and Peter were excited. They gladly got dressed, and even helped their mother pack things. "Where are we going, Daddy?" Jeff, who was seven, asked.

"Maybe to Grandma's," Bill said, although he didn't know . . . only that he felt an irresistible force pulling him inland, away from the coast.

But, still, the weather reports had not changed.

At 10:30 P.M., Bill, Ellen, and the boys drove out of their driveway, and headed west, inland. At midnight, an emergency weather report interrupted normal broadcasting: Hurricane Hazel had changed course. She was heading north and west— right for the northern coast of South Carolina, and Murrell's Inlet.

Hurricane Hazel struck the coast at 2 A.M. In many areas, the storm had knocked down power lines, so that people who depended on the radio for weather news were without it. They were unprepared.

The hamlet of Murrell's Inlet was demolished. Seven people were killed. Of twenty houses and two small commercial buildings, only four houses remained. The hurricane tore the roof off the Collinses' house and hurled it two miles. The inner walls collapsed onto one another. Furniture and belongings were scattered about. No one in the house could have survived.

But, because the man in gray warned Bill Collins about Hurricane Hazel's deadly new course hours before anyone else knew, the Collins family was saved.

The Good-Night Kiss

It looked as if the summer between his freshman and sophomore years in college would be the luckiest time Daryl Williamson ever had known. His grades had been good, so his parents weren't bugging him. His friend Gordo was selling hamburgers at the local fast food joint. But Daryl had gotten a job working for a surveyor. It kept him outside most of the time and he liked that. His uncle had given him a car. It was old, but it was in good shape and didn't look too bad. Everything seemed perfect.

Everything except his love life.

Daryl had never really had a girlfriend. Not that he hadn't tried. Gordo had even tried to fix him up with girls, but Daryl was shy and awkward.

He didn't know what to say or do. It had never worked out. But he had a good feeling about this summer. Everything else was working out just fine. It was time now for a girlfriend.

He was thinking these thoughts as he drove home from a day's work when he saw Christi standing by the bus stop. Christi Morris! Daryl had watched her all through high school. Christi was the kind of girl you couldn't help but notice, a pretty blonde with sparkly blue eyes. She had a smile that just lit up the whole sky. She was silly and a real flirt, but Daryl's heart skipped every time he saw her or even thought about her. The problem was Christi had never noticed him. Had never even spoken to him. She had her eyes on bigger game.

Daryl slowed the car. He could give her a ride, he thought. Why not!

He stopped the car, leaned over and opened the passenger window. "Need a lift?" he called.

Christi looked up and frowned. Daryl felt himself blush. She didn't recognize him.

"Hey, Christi, it's me, Daryl. Remember, high school chemistry?" She should remember, he thought. He had done her lab assignments all year and she had not even thanked him. She had spent her time flirting with other boys.

"Daryl?" She ran over to the car and peeked in. "Hey, Daryl." She opened the door. "Am I glad you came along. I've been waiting forever for that bus."

"Where're you going?"

"Home." She reached over and turned up the volume on the radio. "You listen to this?" It was a radio station that played jazz in between the programs. The truth is that Daryl liked the program, and he liked the jazz too.

Christi changed to a rock station and turned up the volume. The car became a boom box, but Daryl didn't care. Christi Morris was riding in his car. He wanted to drive down every street in town so people could see.

"You take the bus often?" he shouted over the music.

"Yeah. I'm working in Doc White's office over on Bridge Street. I take this bus every afternoon."

"I could pick you up," Daryl said.

"You could? That would be super keen. Can you pick me up tomorrow morning, at eight?"

Daryl really couldn't. He was supposed to report for work at eight. But he couldn't resist. "Sure. Tomorrow?"

"Super."

He dropped Christi off at her house. "Tomorrow at eight. Be on time," she called as she ran up her sidewalk.

Tomorrow. Daryl felt as if he was floating. So he'd be a little late for work. Jake would understand, he hoped.

The next morning Daryl was at Christi's house at five minutes to eight and waited. Finally, at 8:20, she came out and got into his car.

"G'morning," Daryl said.

Christi didn't even look at him. "Step on it or I'll be late."

Daryl dropped her off and then tore over to his job. Jake was understanding. "Just don't let it happen again."

Daryl swallowed hard. "Uh, Jake, I'm going to have to come in after eight. I have to take my mom someplace every morning."

"Can't she leave earlier?"

"No. Sorry."

"Well," Jake mumbled. "Get here as soon as you can."

Daryl felt awful lying, but it was worth it for Christi. This was his year, he was sure of it.

For two weeks, the routine was the same. Daryl would pick Christi up and she was always a little late. Then in the afternoon he'd tear over to Doc White's office and pick up Christi and take her home. She never said thanks, never talked at all. And then one morning she was all sweetness and talk. There was going to be a party out at the Logans' cabin. Just kids, no grown-ups at all, and would Daryl like to go?

Daryl could hardly talk he was so pleased. "Sure," he mumbled.

"Can you drive?" Christi asked.

"Sure."

"Saturday night. Be at my house at eight." She opened the car door. "And wear something decent. Do you have a leather jacket?"

He didn't, but his uncle did. He was sure he could borrow it. "Yeah, sure," he muttered.

"Well, wear it." She got out of the car.

Saturday dragged by. Daryl thought the evening would never come. He was so excited he couldn't eat dinner. He showered and dressed and then sat in the living room waiting until it was time to go. The Logans' cabin! He knew about the Logans. They were the richest family in town. Rick Logan was his age, but he had never paid any attention to Daryl. Now he was going to some expensive Eastern college. Daryl could hardly wait to get to the party.

At eight sharp, Daryl was at Christi's house. She didn't invite him in and he waited on the porch until she and her cousin came out. There were two other girls with them, girls Daryl didn't know.

"My cousin Betts," Christi said. "And Kathy and Mindy. They're from Reed City. Just visiting."

Daryl muttered hellos and the girls piled into the car. They talked and giggled all the way out to the cabin. Not once did they speak to Daryl, but he didn't mind. It was fun just having them in the car. It had begun to rain, a fine mist that made it hard to see.

The cabin was on a country road, but he found it easily. He let the girls out in front and then drove farther down the road to park. The road was wet, and by the time he reached the cabin, his feet were muddy. He scraped his shoes off as best he could, and finally entered the cabin. It was wall-to-wall people. He could hardly move. Everyone was laughing and drinking and talking all at once. Music was blaring and some were trying to dance.

Daryl struggled through the crowd and then he saw Christi. She was leaning against the wall. Rick Logan was standing in front of her, one hand resting against the wall. Christi was laughing.

Daryl walked up to them. "Uh, Christi, let's dance."

Christi jerked her hand away. She looked at Rick and then back at Daryl. "Dance? With you? No way!"

Daryl sucked in his breath. He felt as if he'd just been hit in the gut. "Christi, I thought we had a date."

"A date!" she shrieked. "I wouldn't go out with you if you were the last man on earth. Get lost!" She turned and rushed away.

Daryl couldn't even look around. He knew everyone had heard her. He wanted to die right there on the spot. Slowly, he turned and, without looking to the right or the left, walked outside.

The rain had become harder, and a light

fog was settling in. He stood on the porch for a few moments, gulping air as if he had been drowning. And then a hot rage filled him. He felt his body get warm and he leapt off the porch. Christi wasn't interested in him at all. She had been using him all summer. He must have been blind and deaf not to have seen it. He was just transportation to her, just a car.

Inside his car, he hit the steering wheel with his palms. "Fool!" he shouted. He'd been such a fool. She was probably in there laughing at him with her friends right now. He started the car and spun his wheels as he raced back down the dirt road.

The fog was heavy, thick and white as milk, and he could see only a few feet ahead of the car. He was rounding the corner near Patterson's farm when he thought he saw someone standing at the side of the road. He slowed the car even more and peered through the windshield. The fog and rain made it hard to distinguish, but it looked like a girl. She was dressed all in white, a long flowing dress. Her hair was dark and streamed down her shoulders onto her back. She was like a vision, and then she waved her arm.

Daryl slammed on the brakes and stopped. It was a girl, standing in the rain. He opened his car door and stepped out. "Need a ride?" he called.

She ran to his car. "Oh, yes."

"Get in." Daryl ducked back into the car.

The girl slid into the seat beside him. She was soaked through and shivering. He slipped out of his jacket and held it out to her. "Put this on. You'll catch your death if you don't warm up. I'll get the heater going."

She put the jacket on and then buckled her seat belt. She looked at Daryl and grinned. "Buckle up," she said.

Daryl smiled and buckled his seat belt. "Where are you going?" he asked.

"Home," she said. "I'll tell you how to get there."

He put the car into first and pulled away.

"I suppose you want to know how I got out here," she said.

Daryl was dying to know but had been too polite to ask. "Well, I was sort of wondering. It's a nasty night."

She nodded. "I know. I went to a party with some friends. One of them said he was the designated driver and wouldn't drink, but he did. I didn't know it until we were in the car. I was in back with my boyfriend. My ex-boyfriend," she said and emphasized the "ex" part. "Anyway, my boyfriend started getting very pushy, you know, doing things I said he shouldn't. And then the driver started driving crazy. You know, showing off. Well, I got mad and then scared and told them they had to stop the car right then and let me out."

"Did he? Stop the car?"

She smiled a sad smile. "Oh, he stopped all right. And they pushed me out. They didn't even give me my coat." She shivered. I've been standing out there for hours."

Daryl frowned. He had driven out this road earlier that night and hadn't seen her. But then, he was so excited about Christi he probably wasn't seeing anything right.

"Well," Daryl said. "I haven't been drinking and I won't try anything."

She smiled again. "I know. You're really a good guy."

Daryl blushed. Yes, he was a good guy and what good had it done! He'd acted like a fool over a girl and she had embarrassed him in front of everyone.

The girl reached over and put her hand on his hand. "Don't be embarrassed. It's all right to be good. Sometimes the thrilling things that happen to people when they're bad look exciting. As though you'd like to have those things happen to you."

Daryl nodded.

"Cheap thrills, I call them. It's okay to wait a bit." She squeezed his hand. "Don't worry. Wonderful things will come to you. Just you wait. And the right girl will come along. Maybe not this summer, but soon. Don't give up."

Daryl felt a thrill go through him.

"Oh," she said. "There's my street. Just turn left at the next corner."

Daryl turned and drove down the residential street. "There it is," she said. "The big yellow house on the corner."

He pulled in front of the house and stopped the car. The girl turned to him. "Thank you." She smiled and then quickly she leaned over and kissed him. Right on the mouth.

Before Daryl could recover she had opened the door and gotten out. He watched her run up the steps. At the door she turned and waved, then she went inside. He sighed. His mouth still felt buzzy, the way it did when she kissed him. Slowly, he drove away.

It wasn't until he was almost home that he realized she still had his jacket. No sweat, he thought. He could drive by tomorrow and get it. Maybe she'd go with him to a movie or to have a pizza or something.

His parents were surprised when he came home so early, but he told them the party was boring and he had left. He couldn't tell them about Christi, it was too embarrassing. And he wouldn't tell them about the girl, it was too precious. He didn't even know her name.

He was up early the next morning. Maybe they'd go to church, he thought, and so he whiled away the morning waiting until he could go to her house. He practiced what he would say in front of the bathroom mirror. No more bumbling around as he'd done with Christi.

It was finally one o'clock. "I'm going out,"

he told his parents. He raced to his car and then drove over to her house.

There it was, the big yellow house on the corner. He combed his hair, checked himself in the mirror, and then got out of the car. He rang the bell and waited. A woman opened the door. "Yes?"

"Is your daughter in?" Daryl asked.

The woman gasped. "Oh, no." Tears welled up in her eyes. "Our daughter was killed in an accident out near Patterson's farm a year ago last night. She's buried in the old cemetery near Bateman's Corners." Quickly, she closed the door.

Daryl stood as if he was frozen. Slowly he turned and went to his car. It couldn't be, he thought. She had been so real. And she had kissed him, he had felt that. Mechanically, he drove out to Bateman's Corners.

He found the grave. It was under a huge maple tree in the corner. A shiver ran down Daryl's back and his mouth buzzed, for there, wrapped around the gravestone, was his uncle's leather jacket.

The Girl with the
Deadly Hair

Fanny Leftoe had owned the Happy Hairdo Salon for years. But no one called it the Happy Hairdo. Everyone called it Fanny's.

The kids in the high school were always coming up with new ideas to do things and this year they had a crazy one. The boys were all getting crew cuts and dyeing their hair white. The girls were going to have a bouffant hairstyle contest.

Next thing you knew, no one could get into Fanny's. It was packed wall-to-wall with girls wanting to find out how to do a bouffant style.

Fanny was furious. "You girls will ruin my business. Go on, all of you. Git! I won't have any part of your bouffant business."

The girls went outside and thought about

what to do. Maybe if just one of them went in, Fanny might fix her hair. She could watch and learn what to do and then teach the others. They decided Maribelle should make an appointment for a cut, and then when she got there, ask for the bouffant style. They took up a collection to pay for it and made Maribelle promise she would watch carefully and ask lots of questions. Maribelle agreed. She called Fanny's and made an appointment for Saturday morning, nine-thirty.

Saturday morning, right on time, Maribelle showed up at Fanny's for her appointment. Her friends waited across the street at the drugstore, drinking lime Cokes and reading the magazines and comics.

"Hi, Maribelle," Fanny said. "How's your mother?"

"She's just fine. She was here yesterday for her usual."

"I know, but I like to make conversation with my clients. Helps to relax them."

She shook out a gray and pink plastic apron and spread it over Maribelle's shoulders. "You want a shampoo and set too?" Fanny asked.

"Well, no, not exactly." All the speeches Maribelle had planned flew out of her head and she couldn't think of a thing.

"Come on girl, I've got other customers after you. What will it be?"

Maribelle turned to face her. She took a deep breath. "Well, the guys have all gone and practically shaved their heads and so we girls thought we'd have a contest. A bouffant hairstyle contest. You know, like women used to do."

"Bouffant!"

"Yes. Mr. Crafton, he's our history teacher, got all excited about it because of Marie Antoinette. The women in her day wore wigs with the hair piled so high they could put little boats and things in them. He cut out pictures and put them on the bulletin board. He said he would judge our contest."

Fanny just stood with her mouth open and said nothing.

Maribelle hurried on. "Well, we all have long hair, but we don't know about setting it and curling and stuff. So everyone put money in a collection and sent me in here to find out what to do and I'm supposed to teach them all." She gasped for breath.

Fanny slowly shook her head back and forth. "I want no part of it."

"Oh, Fanny," Maribelle pleaded. "You've got to help. The girls will kill me if you don't."

"Your hair may kill you," Fanny said ominously.

Maribelle's eyes widened. "What do you mean?"

Fanny took the plastic apron off Maribelle. "I've got customers waiting."

"Oh, please." Tears filled Maribelle's eyes.

"Tell you what. You come back with your friends at five tonight. I'll tell you then."

"Oh, thank you, Fanny. Thank you."

Fanny smiled sadly. "I'll see you at five."

Maribelle and her friends were there at five. They brought potato chips and soft drinks. It was like a party.

Fanny was pleased. She opened a soft drink and settled herself in one of her wicker chairs. The girls sat where they could. They all looked at Fanny and waited.

Fanny liked the attention. "Well, I promised Maribelle here that I'd tell her why I don't do a bouffant hairstyle." She sipped from her drink. The room was so quiet you could have heard a pin drop.

Fanny smiled. It was like being on stage. She'd always thought she could have been an actress or a psychologist. She had plenty of practice with her customers. She took a deep breath and began. "Bouffant hairstyles were the rage years ago. Bouffant means 'puffy,' you know, like those crinoline petticoats the girls wore under their poodle skirts."

The girls nodded. Sometimes they dressed like that for Halloween.

"Well, to do a bouffant hairdo, you take all your hair and see how high you can pile it up on your head. Takes a lot of hair spray." She took another sip and looked around at her audience. The girls followed her every move.

"A few years back, the senior girls decided to have a bouffant hair contest. Every girl in town began experimenting, trying to see how high she could get her hair. The drugstore had to put in a special order for hair spray, it got so bad. The prize was going to be fifty dollars and a free dinner at Skogmo's Cafe for two." Fanny gazed off into the distance and her face saddened.

"My niece Betty really wanted to win. She had her eye on Andy Ackerman and she figured with the fifty dollars she could buy a new outfit, maybe two if there was a sale. And she could take Andy out for dinner. Just the two of them." She looked at the girls and smiled. "You know, it would be a romantic evening."

The girls smiled back. They knew.

"Betty came to me in tears. All the other girls were having more luck with their hairdos and she didn't know what to do. She pleaded with me to fix her hair." Fanny shrugged. "What was I to do? She was my niece. And I did know how to make bouffants. I did it nearly every day. So I agreed."

Fanny ate a potato chip slowly.

"Well," Maribelle prompted. "What happened?"

"Betty had the most beautiful dark brown hair you ever say. Had enough hair for two, and it was naturally curly." She sighed. "I'd have given my eye teeth for that head of hair. Most people would have. And it was long. Making a bouffant hairstyle was easy with her hair. And I put some little French braids on the side for effect. It was gorgeous, if I do say so myself.

"For the contest, we put little ribbons in it. Pale blue satin." She sipped her drink slowly.

"What happened?" a girl blurted out.

Fanny smiled. "Oh, she won. She bought the outfits she wanted with the money, a pale blue dress, some new jeans and a sweater. She asked Andy for the date and he said yes. Andy drove his dad's car and picked her up. They drove to Skogmo's Cafe and had shrimp cocktails for appetizers and steaks with baked potatoes. They had Baked Alaska for dessert. It was really special.

"After dinner they went out to the Log Cabin nightclub and danced and then he drove her home. Andy told Betty it was the nicest date he'd ever been on and that she looked just like a picture with her hair piled up like that with those little blue ribbons. And he kissed her, twice. Betty was in heaven."

The girls sighed.

"But it doesn't end there. Betty wouldn't take down her hair."

"She didn't?" Maribelle said. "How did she wash it?"

Fanny looked embarrassed. "She didn't. She just kept spraying it. She said Andy liked it and she wouldn't change it. She did take the blue ribbons out and put others in. And after a while she put silly things in it, little cars and boats. Her friends got used to seeing strange things in her hair. So, no one ever mentioned the spider. They thought Betty had put it there."

The girls shivered.

"And when the little nest appeared, they all thought it was part of the joke and so wouldn't mention it to her. I even saw it and said nothing. We all thought that if we ignored her hair she'd take it down." Fanny sighed. "But she never did."

"What happened?" Maribelle whispered.

"The babies hatched in the night."

"Babies?" one girl whispered. "And . . . ?"

Fanny straightened up. "Betty's mother found her the next morning still in her bed. Her face was all red and purple and swollen up and those little black spiders were all over her—black widow spiders." She shuddered.

"By then there was no way we could get her hair down. They buried her in the pale blue dress with blue ribbons in her bouffant hair."

Fanny looked at the girls. Her eyes were like steel. "And that's why I won't have anything to do with a bouffant hairstyle. No way."

The girls were silent.

Fanny stood up. "Now go on home. And shampoo your heads, every one of you."

Quietly, the girls left.

The following week, Mrs. Olson reported that the drugstore was having a run on shampoo and that girls were returning cans of hair spray. Fanny smiled when she heard it.

The Pond Is Full of Snakes

It had been the hottest summer on record and Mr. Rumson and his boys were still making hay. "You gotta make hay while the sun shines!" Mr. Rumson said.

The Rumson boys were George and Jimmie Boy. George was older and bigger, while Jimmie was small for his age. George was at least a head taller, almost as tall as his pa. And he had a good twenty pounds more weight than Jimmie had. But Jimmie was a hard worker and was keeping up with his pa and George. That made George mad, so he just speeded up.

"I'll keel over if I don't cool down," Jimmie finally said.

"Quit your bellyaching and get to work," George hollered over at him.

Jimmie had only stopped for a second, just long enough to get his wind. George was always bossing him around. Trying to act like some big shot, like he was better than anybody. *He's always showing off*, Jimmie thought. *I can't help it if I'm small. I just got born this way.* But George never let up. He seemed to get some kind of thrill out of picking on Jimmie. George called him a runt. When Jimmie's ma heard that, she reminded Jimmie that the runt of the litter was her favorite. That really made George mad.

"We'll soon be done, boys," Mr. Rumson said. "Then you can go down to the pond for a swim."

"All right!" George called out. "Let's hop to it."

Of course he'd want to go swimming, Jimmie thought. He's got a new suit. Jimmie had to wear George's old one with a patch on the back where George tore it showing off for the Thompson girls over at the river. Sometimes Jimmie wished terrible things would happen to George. Just terrible! Jimmie clenched his teeth and tossed a bale of hay onto the hayrack. He glanced at George, and then whispered under his breath, "I can hardly wait till the day comes when I say 'Good-bye, George, good riddance.'"

"Get a move on, runt," George said, and he poked at Jimmie with the end of a hoe. "I want to go swimming."

Jimmie was hot enough for a swim, but he

wasn't so sure about the pond. His pa had built it last year. It was for the cattle so they could drink out in the far end of the pasture. Pa had used a team of horses to dig into a hill. Then he'd used the dirt to dam up the end. He'd made a right nice hole. And then the rain had filled it up right to the brim. The cows had used it all last summer, mucking around the edges. But this summer had been hot and dry and the pond had started turning a funny brown color. The cows were staying away.

"Hey, half-pint," George called. "Are you going to stand around dreaming all day? Get busy. Pa and I are way ahead of you."

"Drop dead," Jimmie whispered under his breath. *Why is he always on my case?* Jimmie wondered. George was always picking on him. He never picked on Matt, their little brother. It seemed as if he just liked to torment Jimmie. Jimmie sometimes wondered if maybe it was because he was smarter than George. Book learning had been easy for him. He liked reading. He even liked the writing they did for school assignments. But his favorite was making up stories, scary ones about ghosts and monsters and such. They were all about George. How the monsters came and did terrible things to him. Jimmie kept it a big secret. George would kill him if he found out.

Jimmie tossed another bale of hay onto

the hayrack. Someday I'll get even, he thought. Someday.

As Jimmie leaned over to tie the next bale, he saw something wiggling in the straw. He bent down to get a better look. It was a snake. A little brown one. He didn't say anything and sure enough it wriggled right over George's bare foot. Jimmie knew he hated snakes more than anything. One minute George was bending over a bundle of hay and the next thing he was jumping around like a wild man. He let out a bloodcurdling yell and began to wiggle all over. He just stood there, yelling and shaking. It was a sight.

"Kill it, Pa!" he screamed. "Kill it."

"It's just a baby," Jimmie said. "It wouldn't hurt a flea."

"You did this on purpose," George yelled at Jimmie. "I'll get you for this. I'll kill you . . . I'll—"

Pa interrupted. "George, cool down. It's only a small snake."

George picked up a hoe that was nearby and began swinging. "I'll get that evil thing," he screamed and he beat away at the ground. Jimmie tried to get the hoe away from him, but George was bigger and he knocked him down. George chopped with that hoe like a crazy person and soon he got it. He cut the poor little thing right in half. Then he started swinging at Jimmie.

Mr. Rumson grabbed the hoe. "Back to work," he said. "Cut out this foolishness."

"Those snakes are evil," George said. "They oughta all be killed off."

"I kind of like them," Jimmie said. But he said it softly because he didn't want George to hear. If George knew Jimmie wasn't afraid of snakes he'd have a fit for sure.

Jimmie finally finished his last bundle while Pa and George watched. Pa moved once to help, but George stopped him. "He's a big boy now, Pa. You gotta stop babying him."

Pa grinned. "I never babied you boys. Just helped a little now and then. That's what fathers are for." He looked hard at Jimmie. "Well, I'll be. You are growing up, Jimmie Boy. If this keeps up I'll have to start calling you James."

Jimmie smiled. It was a little joke they shared, one George didn't know about. Once when George was being cruel to Jimmie, Pa had found him crying out behind the barn. Jimmie's brand-new Tonka Truck was broken and he knew who had done it. George could break your things and pretend it was an accident, and pinch you where the black and blue marks didn't show. Then he'd lie about it. He was good at that.

"George being hard on you, son?" Pa had asked.

Jimmie nodded.

"He's got a mean streak in him, Jimmie,

my boy. Don't mind him, and when you're grown up, I'll call you James. It was my father's name, you know. A name you can be proud of."

"Why don't you call me James now?" Jimmie had asked. "Then maybe George would leave me alone."

"I call you Jimmie Boy because you are my boy, and I'm mighty glad you are. You've got to get tougher, son, because George may never leave you alone."

Jimmie shivered just thinking about what his pa had said that day. Never was a long time.

George threw a small stone at Jimmie. "Hurry up, squirt. Pa said we could go swimming when we were done. Maybe the Thompson girls will be there. You going to take all night?"

"I'm hurrying," Jimmie said.

"Well," Pa said. "You come up to the house for something cool to drink before you go off swimming. Don't want you to shock your systems and drown."

Jimmie finally finished and followed George up to the house. Their ma had Kool-Aid in a big pitcher. It took two glasses to wash the dryness out of Jimmie's throat.

"You put on your swim trunks now," their ma said. "I don't want you swimming in your clothes."

Jimmie hurried up to his attic bedroom

and got into the old trunks. Then he raced outside.

George was already walking toward the pond. "Hey, wait for me," Jimmie called as he ran. "Pa said you were to wait for me." Pa hadn't really said that, but Jimmie figured he would if he asked him.

George turned and sighed in a dramatic way, as if Jimmie was some kind of pest or something. "Come along, slowpoke. It'll be dark by the time we get there at this rate."

As they came to the top of the hill, Jimmie could see the pond. It was now dark brown and not a cow was in sight.

"I don't like the looks of it," he said.

"Oh, you sissy. You're scared of your own shadow."

"Am not!" Jimmie sputtered. "But why is it so brown? And there are waves. How come? There's no wind."

"Natter, natter, natter. You're worse than some feeble old man. The water's just low, that's all."

George started to run toward the pond, and without even slowing down, he dove in.

Jimmie watched, but George didn't come up. Jimmie held his breath as he waited. He looked the whole pond over and then saw some wild thrashing about and a brown hand and then an arm came up out of the water. And then George's head, all brown and lumpy. "Get Pa!" George shrieked. The water splashed and he started going under again. "Pa!" he gurgled, and then he was gone.

Jimmie turned and headed for home as fast as he had ever run in his life. His feet hardly touched the ground he ran so fast. He was out of breath when he topped the first hill, but he kept on running. He was like the wind. Something awful was happening in that pond.

"Pa!" he screamed as soon as he could see the house. He kept running and yelling and soon saw his pa come out onto the porch. By that time Jimmie was nearly winded. "Pa! George! The pond!"

Mr. Rumson scratched his head and then came down the stairs. Jimmie ran up to him and grabbed his hand and began pulling him toward the pond.

"Son, what's wrong?" Mr. Rumson asked.

"George. Drowning."

Mr. Rumson grabbed a shovel that was leaning against the porch rail and he began to run. His long legs flew over the dry ground. And Jimmie ran right beside him.

When they got to the pond no one was in sight. The water was moving more than ever and it was quiet as death.

"I can't swim," Mr. Rumson said. And he began to dig away at the dirt that dammed the pond. After a few minutes, his hair was plastered to his head and the sweat drained off his face. Jimmie got down and helped, throwing the dirt away with his hands. They worked like they were crazy.

Finally, there was a little trickle of brown water. Mr. Rumson poked at the hole and the dam gave. They jumped out of the way as the water rushed down into the valley.

Mr. Rumson scrambled to the top of the dam and gasped. Jimmie hurried up and stood beside him. There was a body in the bottom of the pond, wet and swollen and covered with the things that had turned the pond a dark brown color—*hundreds of brown twisting, wriggling snakes.*

Where Do Your Stories Come From?

Someone once asked me where my stories come from, and where he could find his own true frights. The answer to both questions is: your local public library. That's where I found most of the stories retold in this book. A few of them came from surfing the Internet and searching archives of magazines and newspapers.

To get you started, I'm going to suggest some books you probably can find in your library. Some events, such as the great Malibu fire or the kidnapping and burial of the young college girl, have been written about at length in books and magazine articles. The sighting of the demon cat of Washington and the Hollywood ghost story appear in books about famous American ghosts. Other tales have been inspired by a single paragraph in a newspaper article, in which case you'll have to imagine what it must have been like for the boy or girl suddenly caught in a terrifying crisis.

At least one tale, the ghost of the Charlton Court, happened to the ancestors of a friend of mine. It is recounted here as it was told to me. That story, like the others, is true, or so it seemed to those who witnessed them.

If you liked these stories, you might want to read the following to experience more "true frights":

Ripley's Believe It or Not—Accidents & Disasters; Coward, McCann & Geoghegan (1982).

Ghosts That Still Walk, Real Ghosts of America, by Warren Chappell; Knopf (1948).

Disaster: Major American Catastrophes, by A. A. Hoehling; Hawthorne Books (1973).

Haunted Houses, by Larry Kettlekamp; William Morrow (1969).

83 Hours Till Dawn, by Gene Miller and Barbara Jane Mackle; Doubleday (1971).